BUTTE FALLS

PETER'S POCKETS

by Eve Rice
illustrations by
Nancy Winslow Parker

Greenwillow Books, New York

For Britt and Bayne
and Wyn and Dale,
the inspiration
for this book
—E. R.

For Alfred and Widdy
—N. W. P.

Library of Congress Cataloging-in-Publication Data
Rice, Eve.
Peter's pockets/by Eve Rice; pictures by Nancy Winslow Parker.
p. cm.
Summary: Peter's new pants don't have any pockets, so Uncle Nick lets Peter
use his until Peter's mother solves the problem in a clever and colorful way.
ISBN 0-688-07241-0.   ISBN 0-688-07242-9 (lib. bdg.)   [1. Pockets—Fiction.]
I. Parker, Nancy Winslow. ill.   II. Title.
PZ7.R3622Pe 1989   [E]—dc 19   87-15640   CIP   AC

Watercolor paints, colored pencils, and a black pen were used for the full-color art.
The text type is Weidemann Book.

One Saturday morning,

Peter put on a pair of brand-new pants. Mama had rolled up the cuffs just right.

"Well, that's a fine pair of pants,"
said Uncle Nick when he arrived.

And Peter said, "I know."

Mama tied Peter's sneakers on tight and said, "See you later. Please don't be late for lunch."

"Okay," said Peter.

Uncle Nick called, "Hey Pete, let's
go to the boat pond!"
It was Peter's favorite place.

So Uncle Nick and Peter walked, and
Peter's pants went *scritch, scritch,*
because they were so new.

Suddenly, Peter stopped.
"A blue feather," he said.
He picked it up.

"Let's take it home," said Uncle Nick.

And Peter would have put it in his pocket but—he couldn't find one anywhere. Not left, not right, not front, not back—

his new pants had *no* pockets!

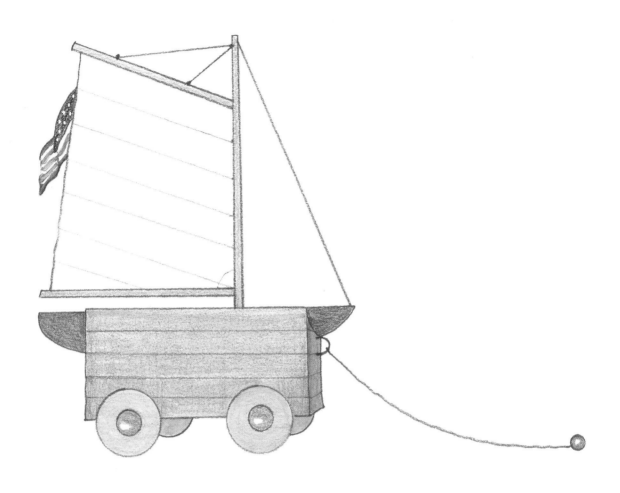

"No pockets? Why that's absurd!" said
Uncle Nick. "But it's okay. You can
borrow mine."
He put the feather in his pocket, and
they went on their way.

Scritch, scritch. And the farther they walked, the more things Peter found— two ribbons, one yellow and one red,

a shiny button,

a ball that bounced,

a marble, and a new nickel—

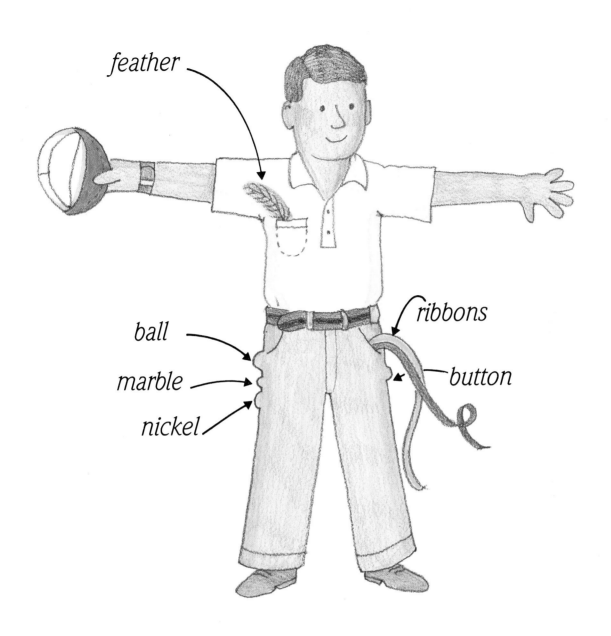

feather

ball

marble

nickel

ribbons

button

and they all went into Uncle Nick's pockets.

When they got home, Uncle Nick and Peter
put everything on the table for Mama to see.
"My, my. What a lot of good things," she said.

Then Peter told her about the pockets.
"No pockets?" Mama said.
"No pockets," said Uncle Nick.

Peter brought out some old pants.
Mama helped him put them on.

Then Peter and Uncle Nick sat down to eat
—but Mama disappeared.

When Peter and Uncle Nick finished lunch,
Mama still had not returned.

"Where is Mama?" Peter asked.

"Wait," said Uncle Nick. "I think I hear
footsteps."

And Mama called, "No pockets? Who ever heard of such a thing!"

Mama held up Peter's new pants. "Here they are." But they didn't look the same at all.

Where Peter's pockets came from:

kitchen curtains
scrap

worn out
gardening jacket

discarded
dish towel

yard-sale
remnant

Grandmother's
old housedress

last year's
bathing suit

Now Peter's pants had big pockets, bright
pockets, *lots* of pockets everywhere.
"See," said Mama. "I've sewn you a pocket
for each good thing you found."

Peter put his new pants on again and
filled his new pockets, one by one.

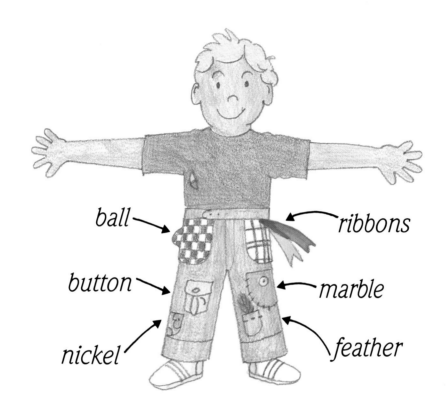

ball →   ← ribbons

button →   ← marble

nickel ↖   ← feather

"There!" Peter smiled and turned all the way around for Mama and Uncle Nick to see.

Mama smiled. "New pants with new pockets."
"And," said Uncle Nick, "they just may be
the finest pants I've ever seen!"